Ace

Nikki Joy

Parson's Porch Books
www.parsonsporchbooks.com

Ace
ISBN: Softcover 978-1-951472-01-6

Cover Credit: Cover illustration by the author's sister, Shana Staton.

Dedication

This story is dedicated to my brother, Nathaniel Staton, who played the characters of Damien and Gev years before they were ever written down on paper. Thank you for being such a good sport, Little Brother!

And also to my God. He's made me who I am today. Without Him, I would be nothing. I am the pen in the hand of my Father. He writes through me. Thank you, Lord.

Prologue

As I sit in my chair, I watch the goings on of the house. My lovely wife, Lindy, is trying to cook dinner. She has splotches of flour here and there, and she makes it look so cute. While I'm studying my wife, Morgan and Chase come running into my view. They are both little whirlwinds, and at the age of seven, they can get into a lot of trouble. Lindy and I have to keep a tight leash on them. Even though we adopted them, they feel just like our own. They may be twins, but they are nothing alike. Morgan is the talkative one. She will talk your ears off if you're not careful, and she's got a mean streak. Chase, on the other hand, isn't as talkative but likes to ask millions of questions that can be difficult to answer. In a few years, Morgan, with here long blond hair and beautiful blue eyes, will probably be turning the heads of all the young boys. Chase has blond hair, green eyes, and a toothy grin making him cute as a button. I love them both so much; sometimes it's hard for me to believe that they're not actually my own flesh and blood.

A knock sounds at the door, and Morgan and Chase race off to answer it. Chase trips over the entry rug and goes sprawling. Morgan reaches a hand out to him, and he yanks her down beside him. The knock comes again, this time more persistent, and the twins are back on their feet. Morgan yanks the door open, and I can tell that whoever it is doesn't stand a chance. Morgan is already talking a mile a minute. Going on about how Chase tripped, and she won. I hear something about new shoes and decide to rescue whoever it is. I go to the door and pull my younger brother, Gev, inside. He just returned from Air Force training, so I'm glad to see him again. It has been nearly a year since I saw him last. The twins are ecstatic that they're Uncle Gev is finally here. They are both clamoring for his attention as Lindy calls us into the kitchen for dinner. We all head that way, the twins racing out ahead of Gev and I. "It's good to see you brother." I say, clapping him on the shoulder before we get seated at the kitchen table. He gives me a lopsided grin in response. Once we are all seated, it becomes painfully obvious that someone is missing. Three-year-old Arthur walks in and takes his seat. The twins snicker, and Gev's eyes cloud over with grief. Lindy hushes the twins and pats Arthur comfortingly on his little hand. The prayer is said, and supper continues in companionable silence.

Lindy puts out a nice spread of chicken, mash potatoes, macaroni, and buttered rolls. Morgan looks over at Arthur then elbows Chase. I know something hateful is fixing to come out of her mouth. She darts a quick look at me, and I give her a stern shake of my head. My warning goes unheeded as she looks at Arthur and says, "Hey Uncle Gev, you want to play basketball after we eat?" Before Gev can say anything, Arthur bursts into tears and runs out of the room. Chase grabs Arthur's hardly touched plate of food and begins eating it. Morgan is giving her famous Cheshire grin, and Gev is sitting with a stunned expression on his face.

Lindy turns to me and says, "Joey, could you please go check on Arthur?" I calmly get up from the table and grab Morgan and Chase by their ears, and ignoring their cries of protest, I drag them into the living room and plop them unceremoniously down on the couch. As calmly as I can, I demand for them not to move an inch. Gev walks in from the kitchen and promises to watch them. I go up the stairs and to the end of the hall where Arthur's room is.

His door is standing wide open, and he is curled up in a ball on his bed. I take a minute to study him. His hair is so black that it almost has a blue tinge to it. He's so small even for a three-year-old. I clear my throat and sit down on the edge of his bed. Arthur sits up beside me, and when I look down, bright blue eyes rimmed by wire-framed glasses are glistening back at me. He looks so much like Ace my heart breaks a little each time I look at him. I fight back my own emotions before I say anything. I put my arm around him and draw him closer to my side. He lays his head against me still looking at me with those eyes, and I nearly lose it. When he says, "I miss my daddy," and a tear leaks out of his eye, my tears come too. I pull myself together enough to get out that I miss him too, and that he was a good man. I don't know how long we sit there like that, but Lindy soon comes in with Arthur's food, and I leave her to it.

Back in the living room, I have the twins to deal with. They are still sitting where I left them looking agitated and apprehensive. I sit down in between them and place my arms across their shoulders. I start out by telling them that being intentionally mean is wrong and not very Christ-like. I don't think I am having any luck getting through to them, though. I decide that a story might help them to understand a bit better. I call up to Arthur, knowing that this is one story that he'll want to hear. I can hear him walking upstairs, and soon he appears in the living room. I give him my seat and pull up a chair for myself. Gev gets up like he's about to leave, and I give him a look that has him sitting back down in a hurry. Lindy comes in from the kitchen and takes a seat next to me. She grasps my hand firmly in show of moral support. She knows that this story isn't going to be easy for me. I clear my throat and falter a moment, not knowing the right place to begin. Finally,

I decide that the very beginning is as good a place as any and plunge in.

Chapter 1

22 years in the past

I watch my dad closely. Ever since Mom died three years ago, he has been rapidly declining. He is constantly losing jobs, and he looks like a stick with a face. Honestly, I think the only thing he puts into his body is beer. I may only be ten, but I can tell he is trying to drown his grief in the stuff. He isn't the only one still grieving though. Seven-year-old Gev just mopes around the house. On this particular day, he has locked himself in his room. I can hear him crying as I pound on the door. He senses that Dad isn't quite right even at his age. Three-year-old Benjamin comes out of his room next to Gev's. Dad comes in downstairs slamming the front door. I can smell the alcohol on him from up here. "Get down here you no good bunch of idiots!" He bellows. Benji and I race down the stairs, and we hear Gev right behind us. Dad is in one of his moods. When he gets in his moods, we know to do what we're told with no questions or hesitation. Today is no different. We all come to a screeching halt in front of him. The stench of alcohol is rolling off of him in waves. He pushes us out of the way and staggers to the couch. We follow obediently behind him. Once he is situated on the couch, he turns to us. His beady eyes swivel and lock on to Benji. He glares with undisguised hatred. He blames Benji for Mom's death. She died giving birth to him. "What did you do today, boy?" He practically growls. Benji keeps his eyes averted. "Look at me when I'm talking to you!" Dad yells at him. I inwardly cringe. Gev grabs my hand. Benji starts to cry. "Get out of my sight, all three of you!" Dad shouts. Gev grabs Benji's hand, and we race up the stairs. I pull them both into my room, and Benji collapses into my arms crying hysterically. I don't know what to do for him, so I awkwardly pat his back.

Finally, after what seems like hours, his cries fade away. He looks up at me like I have all the answers. I wish he wouldn't look at me like that because I never know what to tell him. He is only three years old, too young to know the truth. I do the only thing that I know how and grab a basketball off the floor. We slowly creep back downstairs and out the front door, the task made easier by the fact that Dad is sleeping off his drunkenness. As I throw the ball through the hoop, I feel my tensions draining away. Gev steals the ball from me and shoots and misses. Benji giggles which is a rare sound to hear and gets me started too. Before I know it, all three of us are laughing so hard that tears are streaming down our faces. A car pulls up in the neighbor's driveway, and little Miss Susie gets out of the backseat. She looks our way and sticks her tongue out at us. That gets us all started laughing again. I can hear Susie stomping her foot in disgust in the background. It's feels good to just be little boys for once.

It's been two weeks since the incident with Dad, and he has been more distant than usual. We all have to tip toe around him so as not to have a repeat of two weeks before. We don't talk to him, and he rarely talks to us. Every day I have to go to school and leave Benji alone at the house. We can no longer afford a babysitter or daycare. I tell him to stay inside and not mess with the stove or anything else dangerous, but I still worry about him. I've skipped school three days this week, but I always make sure Gev gets on the bus. Dad has stopped caring one way or the other. He is only a shell of the man he once was. Mom held our little family together, so when she died our family died with her. We may have only lost our mother, but it seems like we're losing our dad too.

Mom was a big fan of church. She told me once that she wanted to watch me grow into a good Christian man. She wanted that for all of us I'm sure. Dad no longer takes us to church, so it is up to me as usual. Every Sunday I help my little brothers dress in the best clothes we own, and we walk down to the church at the end of our street. Today is Sunday, so when Benji comes into my room in a holey t-shirt and a pair of ratty shorts, my mouth falls open. He explains that it is all that he has clean. I guess it is past time for a trip to the laundry mat which also falls on me. I take his hand and head down the stairs. Gev is already waiting at the front door. His clothes don't look any better, in fact they might actually look worse than Benji's. I sigh in resignation. There is nothing that I can do about it now. We'll just have to go as we are and hope no one notices. As we walk into the church twenty minutes late, everyone turns to see who it is. I usher my brothers quickly forward and take a seat on the very back pew. Thankfully, everyone loses interest in us quickly, and the service goes on as usual. As I listen to the preacher speak about how as Christians our duty is to help the poor and needy, I can't help but think that he is talking about us when he says poor and needy. When I look up from my Bible, my suspicions are confirmed by the preacher's kind eyes on me. When the service is over, I try to hurry my brothers out the door before anyone can ask questions. Though, before we can get there, a firm hand on my shoulder halts our progress. I turn reluctantly and look up into the gentle and wise eyes of Preacher John or just Preacher as he is fondly known as. "Would you boys please come to my office for a moment?" Preacher asks. I know this can't be good, but I lead my brothers after the man anyways. As I walk up the aisle pulling my brothers along with me, I can feel eyes on me. We step into

Preacher's office, and he walks to the closet and pulls out a box. "The church wanted to do something nice for you boys, so for the past two weeks members have donated the items in this box. I wanted to personally give it to you." Preacher says as he sits the box down on the floor so that we can all see into it. On top is a book about Fire engines. Benji immediately grabs it up. He is going through the Fireman phase. Every little boy, at least once in their life, wants to be a firefighter. The rest of the box is filled with clothes of all sizes. I can't find the words to express how much it means to me, so I just smile my gratitude and turn to leave.

Back at the house, I find myself putting the box into Dad's beat-up old car. I really can't say what influenced me to do it. I just feel like it's going to be most useful there. As I slip the box into the car, Dad comes out the door. He tells us to get in the car. "I'm taking ya'll for ice cream." He tells us. He's lying, I can tell. We don't have the money to spend on ice cream, and if we did, he would probably be using it on beer not ice cream and certainly not on us, especially since he lost his job again a few days ago. I think to myself that this is it. The day I've known would come eventually. We've passed four ice cream shops already, and he hasn't stopped yet. After a while, we leave the city behind us. I know there are no ice cream shops out here. Gev looks at me, and I can tell that he is thinking the same thing that I am. Dad turns down a long driveway. The house comes into view, and the sign out front reads, "Maxwell Boy's Home." I thought so. Gev looks at me, and knowing he can read my lips, I mouth, "I knew it." Gev just shrugs his shoulders and turns to Benji. He whispers something into his ear, and I see Benji glance at me. I can see the terrified look in his eyes, and I have nothing to say to dispel it. My worst nightmares have come true.

Chapter 2

"Get out of the car." Dad says without yelling or growling. There is no hint of menace in his voice. It is totally dead. It is so uncharacteristic of him that we all just sit there. "I said, get out!" This time he shouts it. I open my door and grab the box out of the floorboard. We are all out in a matter of seconds, and he drives away without even so much as a backward glance. I stand there with Gev on one side and Benji on the other side. When I look down into Benji's bright blue eyes, I see more questions I can't answer there. All I can do is shrug my shoulders. He holds his tiny hand out to me, and I take it. I look down at him one more time, and the questions have been replaced by a pool of tears. My heart breaks. I try to hold it together as we walk up to the front door, but it is far from easy. I ring the doorbell. We stand there for what seems like hours, but in all reality, it has only been minutes. Finally, the door opens. We are ushered inside by a plump, blond-headed lady wearing bright red lipstick and an apron. Gev giggles, and I try to elbow him but fail. Carrying a box makes it hard to do. The lady takes us into a little waiting area. We are told to sit, and then she shuffles off.

"We're not getting any ice cream, are we?" Benji asks in a small voice.

Before I can say anything, Gev says sarcastically, "Well of course we are. This is the new ice cream shop, didn't you know? What else would we be sitting here waiting for? The waitress will be here to take our order any minute now."

At that moment, a man comes up to us. He "invites" us into his office, and again we are seated. He begins by introducing himself as Luke Maxwell, owner of the "Home" as he affectionately calls it. Then he starts asking us questions about ourselves. From our answers he gathers: Our names being Joey, Gev, and Benjamin, Our Dad dropped us off here, and the box of clothing came from Preacher John and the congregation of Helpful Hands Church of God. When he finishes, he hits the intercom button asking for a Mrs. Collins to come to his office immediately. Within seconds, the same lady that let us in, comes into the office. The office seems to shrink at her entrance, and I begin to feel claustrophobic.

Mrs. Collins is asked to escort us to our rooms and leads us out of the office and down the hall. She points out several bathrooms along the way as well as the dining room, classrooms, rec room, and Study Hall. Finally, we get to the living quarters. Off of the main hallway are three more hallways. Each hallway is labeled. We bypass the first hallway labeled, 13-18. The second hallway is labeled, 7-12, and this one we go down. We stop at the second door on the right and she knocks. A young boy Gev's age answers it. Mrs. Collins introduces him as Glover and announces that he is going to be Gev's roommate. I sit the box down and dig around until I find some clothes that will fit Gev and hand them to him. We leave Gev there and continue down the hallway. We reach the last door on the left, and she knocks. This time a boy my age answers the door. Mrs. Collins introduces him as Leon, and my new roommate. Benji has yet to see his new room and roommate, and I can't leave him until I know that he's going to be okay. Benji grabs my hand and looks up at me pleadingly. He doesn't want me to leave him yet either. Mrs. Collins sees all of this and kindly invites me to join them on the trip to Benji's room. Back at the beginning of the hallway, we turn down the last hall marked, 1-6. As we walk down the hall, I count how many doors we pass. We stop at door number 8. There are only two doors left down the hall. Mrs. Collins takes out a key and unlocks the door. We all step inside. The walls are painted a baby blue. There are two beds, and one is unmade. A chest sits open at the foot of the unmade bed. Toys are spilling out of it. "The kids on this hall are having play time right now." Mrs. Collins informs us.

I walk over to the made bed and begin pulling clothes from the box. I leave Benji's clothes and fire engine book in the box. I leave the box sitting on the floor and motion Benji over. I squat down to his level, and he throws himself into my arms. "It's going to be okay. We're going to be okay." I try to reassure him as much as myself. He steps back from my arms and Mrs. Collins and I go to leave. When I look back over my shoulder at Benji, tears are silently streaming down his face. He stands there watching us leave, and I nearly double over in pain. My heart breaks a little bit more.

I have been hanging out in my room since we got here. My roommate, Leon, is okay. He has been trying to engage me in conversation, but I'm trying to ignore him. His questions are never ending, so when a bell rings and he exclaims, "That's dinner," I inwardly breathe a sigh of relief. I follow him to the dining hall. Kids of all ages and sizes are already streaming through the doors. I can't see either of my brothers yet. I wait through a long line of kids to get my trey, and still following Leon, I take a seat. More kids my age sit down around me, and Leon begins to introduce them.

There are four long tables, and like the hallways, they are labeled by age. My table is the third one. On one side of my table are the older kids, and on the other side are the younger kids. I look for Benji but can't see him. I see Gev sitting at the end of my table, and he is laughing and talking with some other boys his age. On the other side of the older kids is the adult table. I see Mr. Maxwell and Mrs. Collins. I turn my attention back to my food and take a bite. Leon clears his throat, and I look up to realize that no one else is eating. Mr. Maxwell stands and says, "Everyone please bow your heads and join hands."

The first boy on the older kids table speaks up saying, "Thank you for this food."

The next boy continues, "And this day." I realize we are doing a popcorn prayer, and I'm going to have to say something.

Before I know it, they are on my table. I hear Gev say, "Thank you for new friends."

It's soon my turn. I flounder only a moment before saying, "Thank you for my brothers." As they get around to the younger kids, I listen for Benji's voice. Just when I decide that I missed it, I hear him say, "Please watch over me."

Throughout the meal I glance at Benji. He isn't eating, and he isn't talking to any of the boys around him. This worries me.

Chapter 3

After dinner, we all make our way to Study Hall. This room is set up much like the dining room, but there are only three tables. These tables aren't labeled, and Leon tells me that I'm allowed to sit with whomever I want. I look around for Gev and Benji. Neither has made it in yet. I wait by the door. When Gev walks through, I grab his arm. I pull him against the wall beside me. I turn back to the door, but some lady is shutting it and telling everyone to take a seat. I sit down beside Leon and pull Gev down beside me.

I look around for Benji but don't see him. Leon notices me looking around and asks who I'm looking for. I tell him my little brother. "He's three." Gev adds.

"Kids that young don't come to study hall. It's only for school age boys." Leon explains. "Each age group has their own play time, but at 7:00 p.m. it's free play. Everyone gets to have a break. You can go outside or to the rec room. You can see your little brother then." Leon tells me.

Everyone is now sitting and pulling out pencils and notebooks. Leon tells me it is homework time, but Gev and I haven't started classes yet. Before I can ask Leon what we are supposed to do, I feel a hand on my shoulder. I turn in my seat to see the lady who shut the door standing behind me. "My name is Ms. Kandy, and I would like to welcome you boys to Maxwell Boys Home. I am head of Study Hall." She tells Gev and I. She hands us both a piece of paper. "These are your schedules, starting tomorrow." She explains. After she is gone, I help Leon with his math. Before I know it, the bell is ringing for free period. Gev goes off with some of his new friends, and I go in search of Benji.

I look in the rec room first, but he isn't there. Next, I head outside. He isn't on the playground, and he isn't playing basketball. I don't see him anywhere. I then decide to check his room. The hallway is eerily quiet. I count to the eighth door and knock. A boy with mousy brown hair and big brown eyes answers the door. "Um hi, I'm Joey. I'm looking for my little brother, Benji. Do you know where he is?" I ask him.

"You're Benji's brother? My name's Damien. Your brother doesn't talk much. He left when the bell rang." The kid tells me excitedly. I smile and turn to leave, but Damien stops me by slipping his hand into mine. He smiles up at me saying, "I'll help you find him."

As we walk back down the hall, I practically get the kids whole life story. He is three, fixing to be four. He came to Maxwell's as a baby. No one wants to be his friend because he talks too much. He has no brothers or sisters that he knows of, and he loves, loves, loves French fries. By the time we make it outside, I'm completely exhausted just from listening to him. I suggest we split up, but he stubbornly clings to my hand. He drags me all over the giant yard and then down to the basketball court. I soon realize that this place has just about everything. One group of boys is playing a game of baseball, while several younger kids are on the playground. Some older boys are shooting hoops. I want to join them so badly, but I can't abandon my search for Benji.

Beside me, I feel Damien tremble. Before I can ask him what's wrong, a basketball hits me in the head. I am lifted off the ground by my shirt front and thrown to the ground. My vision is swimming, and I can't seem to focus on anything. I try to get up, but the guy has his foot on my chest. Thankfully, I feel his foot leave my chest, and I am helped to my feet. "You alright man?" Leon asks, full of concern. There is a crowd of onlookers. I look back at Leon to see if he can tell me what just happened. He points to a big guy who steps menacingly toward me. I take a quick step back.

"You're lucky you're new here, or I would have pummeled you for sure. No one is allowed to step foot on my court unless invited by me." The giant declares.

Leon gives me an apologetic look and backs into the throng of onlookers. The crowd disperses after a minute, and I am left alone with the giant. He points a finger at me and says, "You've been warned, pipsqueak. Now scram!" I take off like a shot. I no longer want to play basketball, at least not with that guy around.

I feel a small trembling hand slip into mine, and I look down to see Damien. "His name is Bruce. I'm sorry I didn't warn you about him. It's just that he scares me, and I panicked." He says quietly.

I smile down at him to put him at ease and pat him reassuringly on the head. "No hard feelings." I tell him with forced cheer. I look around for Benji, and I spot Gev on the playground. Before I can make my way over to him, the bell rings. I pull out my schedule to see what this bell is for. The next thing on the schedule is at 8:30 p.m. which are showers for boys twelve and under. I drop Damien's hand and take off for the front doors.

Showers? I don't even know where the showers are. I follow the other boys into the building. Somehow, I end up with Damien's hand back in mine, and he is pulling me along. "I've found him! I've found him!" He excitedly shouts. Suddenly he stops, and there sits Benji. He's sitting on a bench outside the bathrooms.

Boys are streaming through the bathroom doors, and then I notice that there are three of them. Just like the hallways, they are labeled by age. This place is very organized.

Damien sits down on the bench beside Benji and pats the spot between them for me to sit. "I've never taken a shower before, Joe." Benji states with a tinge of desperation in his voice. "Don't worry, I'll help you." I tell him matter-of-factly. I take his hand in mine, and together we walk into the bathroom labeled 7-12. This place is going to take some getting used to, but I'm sure with time, it won't seem so bad.

Chapter 4

We have been living at Maxwell Boys Home for four months now. Every day I watch my brothers closely. Gev is thriving here. He laughs and plays with the other boys his age. Gev is happier here than he ever was with Dad, and for that I am grateful. Benji, on the other hand, is failing. He talks to no one, not even me. He doesn't participate in anything. He stays in his room all day, even for meals. Every day I bring him his meals, and he barely touches them. He is getting too thin, and he is ghostly pale. I don't know what to do for him. I try to get him to eat, but he mostly refuses or just picks at it. The adults don't know what to do either, and I believe that they have given up.

Today is Sunday. I am alone in my room racking my brain for a solution to Benji's problem when a knock sounds at my door. I open the door to find Benji standing there. He is dressed in a nice pair of dress pants and a polo shirt. "We go to church." He declares.

I pull him into my room and shut the door. I sit him down on my bed and get at eye level with him. "We can't go to church, Benji. We aren't allowed to leave here." I try to explain to him.

"But, Joey, I need to see God. I need to see him now. He's left me, and I need to go find Him. Please Joey." Benji pleads in a small hysterical voice. Tears start to drip from his beautiful blue eyes, and it nearly does me in.

I grab both of his hands in mine and state firmly, "God would never leave you, Benji. He is trying to hold on to you, but you are letting go of His hand. You don't have to go to church to find Him either, He is always right beside you."

By now, tears are streaming down my face too. I try to dash them away, but they just keep falling. Benji's tears have stopped, and he reaches his little hand up to my face and wipes away my tears. "Okay Joey." He says simply. He jumps down off the bed and is out the door before I can say anything else.

It has been three days since having that conversation with Benji, and I have yet to see him. The dinner bell rings, and I make my way to the dining hall. As we go around the room thanking God for things, I hear a small, unsure voice say, "Thank you for giving me Joey." I burst into tears, which is totally embarrassing, and the room goes quiet around me. I feel a small hand pat my back, and I turn to see Benji. He throws himself into my arms and whispers, "It's okay, Joey. It's okay."

Chatter resumes and Benji plops down into my lap. He begins to eat my food. I let him have it.

That same day during free period, Benji finds me in the yard. He hands me his fire engine book and demands me to read it to him. I read it once, twice, three times before he is satisfied. He then demands me to teach him how to read it. I begin teaching him the basics: the alphabet. Every day during free period for two weeks, I teach him the ins and outs of reading. By the end of the second week, he is reading the fire engine book to me all by himself without even a little bit of help from me. It is on that day that I realize that Benji is a very fast learner.

Two days after that, an announcement is made during free period. Mr. Maxwell comes over the loudspeaker and says, “We are taking a trip to the Library. If anyone is interested, meet me in the driveway.” Benji takes off toward the driveway. I run to catch up to him. Several other boys are already there. A bus is sitting a few feet away, and boys are already loading up. Mr. Maxwell is counting each boy as they get onto the bus. I am the last in line, and Benji is already getting onto the bus. After about a minute, I’m the last one still waiting to get on. Mr. Maxwell counts me as number twenty-one and says, “Sorry son, twenty is our max. You’ll have to wait until the next trip.” Benji comes down the steps and pulls at my hand trying to get me to hurry up. I look pleadingly at Mr. Maxwell, and he silently lets me pass.

At the library, the librarian talks to us for a few minutes about checking out books, and then we are dismissed to look around. After the others have moved off, Benji approaches the librarian. I stay back to watch what he will do. He holds out a book to her. I take a step closer to see what book it is. It's his fire engine book, and he's asking her if there are more books like it. She says something in a conspiratorial whisper and takes his hand. She leads him to the children's section and down an aisle marked nonfiction.

I follow along behind them. I can hear Benji telling the librarian all about his fire engine book. Benji stops and pulls a book off the shelf. I move closer to see that it is a book about tigers. He begins to pull more books from the shelf. They are about everything from the different animals to cars and sports. Before he can pull any more books from the shelf, the librarian halts him by saying, "Only ten at a time, remember." He eyes the books he already has out, and then the shelf. He already has more than ten, and so he puts three of them back. He grabs one more off the shelf and adds it to his growing pile. He tries to carry them all but ends up dropping more than half of them. I pick up the rest of them, and he leads me to a table. We plop the books down, and he spreads them all out. His eyes come alive with excitement as he looks at all the books. "1, 2, 3… 8, 9, 10." He counts them excitedly. I have never seen my brother so animated. He claps his hands with glee and opens up a book about kittens. He begins to read aloud to me.

By the time the others are ready to go, he has read it four times already. Before I get in the checkout line with the others, I run back to the nonfiction section and grab ten more books. Benji has already checked out with his new library card and waiting with the others. I'm last, again. I plop my books on the counter and sign my library card. The librarian puts my books in a bag, and we are on our way. "I got these for you, Benji." I tell him once we are seated on the bus. His face lights up and he gives me a big hug. I love this kid.

About a week later, Benji comes running up to me. "It's my birthday." He declares in a sing song voice. I clap my hand to my forehead. I completely forgot about his birthday. "Can we have a party?" He asks. I don't know what they do for birthdays here, so I tell him I will talk to Mr. Maxwell about it.

I head to Mr. Maxwell's office as soon as Benji scampers away. I knock on Mr. Maxwell's door, and it is immediately opened. Mr. Maxwell motions me to have a seat. "What can I do for you, Joey?" He inquires.

"Well, you see sir, it's my little brother, Benji's birthday today, and he really wants to have a party." I tell him hopefully.

Mr. Maxwell jumps from his seat declaring, "Why, that's a splendid idea! You just leave everything to me."

I find Benji and tell him the good news. "Can we invite Preacher John?" He asks me. I turn around and head back to Mr. Maxwell's office.

Once there, I tell him what Benji wants. He declares it another splendid idea and summons Mrs. Collins to his office. "Take this boy to find Preacher John right away." He instructs her.

Mrs. Collins and I get into her nice little car, and I give her directions to Helpful Hands Church of God. As we drive down my old street, unpleasant memories crowd my mind. Mom crying out in agony as she is having Benji; Dad stomping around the house smelling of alcohol and cursing at no one in particular; Gev crying himself to sleep every night; me at the age of eight trying to change two-month-old Benji's dirty diaper, but there isn't a clean diaper in the house; Benji, Gev, and I walking down this very street every Sunday morning in our holey clothing; Benji, Gev, and I walking through the door of Helpful Hands Church of God, and everyone turning and staring; and finally the last memory I have before I shut them down is Dad slapping Benji for no reason at all. Tears begin coursing down my cheeks.

Mrs. Collins pulls into the church parking lot and shuts off the car. "You alright," she asks.

"Just a short trip down memory lane," I manage to get out. I didn't realize how hard this would be. I open my door and say, "Let's go get this over with."

Chapter 5

Benji's birthday party is a huge success. Preacher John gives him a toy fire engine, which he adores, and a Bible to call his very own. Damien hands him a big black teddy bear declaring that it matches his hair. On our way back from seeing Preacher John, I convinced Mrs. Collins to stop at the store. I had fifteen dollars saved, and I bought Benji a giant book about animals of the world. When he opens my present, he loves it. After the party is over, he goes around hugging and thanking everyone for the gifts. When he gets to me, he throws his arms around me and whispers, "Thank you Joey. The book is my favorite."

The next day during free period, Benji sits down on the grass beside me. "Did you know that in the winter, the Artic Hare's fur is white for camouflage; in summer, its fur is brown. Also the largest spider in the world is the Goliath Bird-eating Spider of South America." He informs me.

"Cool. You're an ace." I tell him. Every day after that, he has a new interesting fact to tell me.

#

Day after day goes by until we have been here almost two years. My brothers and I have all gotten older. I am now twelve, and Gev is nine. Benji is six and in school. His teachers are amazed by how fast he learns. He finishes way before all the other kids in his class, and he is allowed to help other students once he is done with all of his work. He is good at every subject, but his favorite is math. One day during Study Hall, I am working on my math homework and am having trouble on a couple of problems. I ask Leon for help, but he declares that he doesn't know how to do them either. Benji is sitting beside me. I watch in amazement as he looks at the lesson, and then he begins to work out the problems that neither Leon nor I could figure out. I call Ms. Kandy over, and she verifies that Benji's answer is correct. Once she is gone, I look at Benji in utter amazement. He really is an ace. "Your name should be Ace." I tell him, and from that day forward Benji is known as Ace.

A week or so later, during free period, Ace shows me a book on how to play basketball. "Teach me." He demands. I tell him no remembering that the basketball court is off limits because it belongs to Bruce. He goes sulking off.

A few weeks later once more during free period, I hear a blood curdling screech. Boys from all directions go running toward the basketball court. Damien comes panting up to me from that direction, and pointing toward the court, he manages to get out between breaths, "A-Ace," in a shaky voice.

I fly toward the court on feet of dread, and the crowd parts to let me through. What I see makes my blood chill. Giant Bruce has tiny Ace pinned to the ground. Bruce is sixteen, more than twice Ace's age. "Leave him alone!" I shout.

"Or what," Bruce sneers.

I can't think straight, and I am seeing red. I charge and ram my shoulder into his side. He is knocked sideways off of Ace, and he lands with a thud on the ground. He jumps up and stalks toward me menacingly.

"Wait!" Ace shouts.

Bruce turns back toward him and grits out, "What?"

"I challenge you to a game of basketball. If my team wins, then the court will no longer belong to you. If your team wins, then you can keep the court." Ace declares. Bruce contemplates it for a moment, and then he reluctantly agrees. "Teams of five," Ace announces.

I don't know what he is thinking. He doesn't even know how to play basketball the last I checked. I tell him this, and he just smiles. Leon, Damien, Gev, and I all volunteer to be on Ace's team. All of Bruce's teammates are his age and way bigger than us. We don't even stand a chance.

At that moment, Mr. Maxwell walks from the gathered crowd of onlookers. "An excellent idea boys, a game is just what we need to liven things up a bit around here. We will invite everyone to watch." He declares with enthusiasm and marches off. A few minutes later, he comes over the loudspeaker announcing, "A basketball game will commence on the court in ten minutes and everyone is to attend." Boys and teachers pour from the building. Mr. Maxwell returns and directs everyone who isn't playing to have a seat on the grass. "Let the Game begin!" Mr. Maxwell shouts. He flips a coin, and Ace calls heads. "Heads it is." Mr. Maxwell announces. It's our ball.

I throw the ball in to Ace, and he takes it down the court. Bruce pops up in front of him and tries to steal the ball. Ace bounces it between Bruce's legs to me. I have a clear shot and take it. I shoot and score. I get high-fives from my teammates, and a glower from Bruce. Bruce takes the ball down the court, and Ace runs at him from the other direction. I don't even see it happening, but somehow Ace has the ball. He has it through the net before anyone can make it back across the court. The score is four to nothing. We are in the lead. The onlookers cheer for Ace, and Bruce grabs the ball angrily from his hands. Bruce starts down the court again, and the ball is snatched right back out of his hands by Ace. I'm closest to our net, so Ace passes the ball to me. I shoot and score. Cheers erupt form the grass. The game continues until we are tied at eighteen. It's our ball. Damien takes it down the court and passes it off to Leon. Leon shoots and is packed by one of Bruce's goons. The ball goes rolling. Ace reaches it first and picks it up. Bruce is coming at him fast. He looms over Ace. Ace fakes a shot. Bruce jumps to block him, and Ace runs underneath him. He shoots a long shot, and everyone holds their breath. "Please let it go in." I silently pray. The ball swishes through the net, and the crowd goes absolutely wild. We won, and I can't believe it. Ace has never played a game of basketball in his life, and he played better than anyone else.

After everyone has dispersed, I turn to Ace and ask, "How did you do that? Who taught you how to play so good?"

He just smiles and says, "I'm an ace remember. I learned how to play ball just like I learn everything else. I learned from a book." He holds up the "How to Play Basketball" book and I look at him in wonder. I realize something else then, my little brother has been blessed with a great gift.

Chapter 6

Another year at the Home has come and gone, and several things have changed. We are each another year older, and Ace has become even smarter. He has learned to play just about every sport including basketball, baseball, soccer, and football. Basketball is his favorite though. Every day he and I shoot hoops during free period. He has become about a thousand times better than me. Every time he shoots, he usually makes it in. If he misses, he is extremely hard on himself. He will keep shooting until he makes it from that spot. Ace is very persistent. He keeps at something until he has it mastered. He is currently teaching himself how to play the guitar. He has gotten pretty good at it.

Bruce has turned eighteen. He left the Home a couple of months ago. Now that he is gone, everyone breathes more easily. My roommate, Leon, got adopted last week. He was my only real friend, besides Ace and Gev, at the Home. I miss him tons. The room feels empty without him. Ace moved into a room on my hall, but I moved too. I now stay in the first room on the left down the first hall, labeled 13-18. Leon was staying in the same room as me before he was adopted.

Today is a beautiful, sunny day. Ace and I are relaxing on the grass after shooting some hoops. It's Sunday, so it is free period all day. Damien joins us on the grass after getting a drink from the water fountain. A car pulls up in the driveway. A young couple, probably no older than twenty-five, exits the car. Mr. Maxwell comes out of the building and greets them. A little boy around three gets out of the back. Mr. Maxwell talks to them a moment and then goes back inside. The couple glances around, and their eyes land on us lying in the grass.

Someone is getting adopted today.

They approach us. The little boy holding his daddy's hand waves at us. We don't return the gesture. As they get closer, we all jump from the ground. The lady, smiling says, "Hello boys. My name is Lillian Marter, and this is my husband Cliff and son Lewis."

"Hi!" Little Lewis pipes up, "I'm three."

I start to walk away, but Ace grabs my hand, stopping me. I turn back to face the little family. Cliff looks each of us over good and then turns to his wife and points at me. I hear him whisper, "That one's too old." He then points at Ace and says something that I can't hear. They turn back to us and pointing at Ace say, "How would you like to come and live with us?"

Ace slowly begins to shake his head no saying, "Unless you take my brothers too then I can't."

The couple shakes their heads and begins to walk away. I reach out to stop them, and they turn back around. Grabbing Damien, I thrust him forward declaring, "He's not our brother. Why don't you take him? He's a good kid." Damien looks up at me with a scared look on his face, and I smile reassuringly down at him.

The man looks at Damien and asks, "Would you like that?" Damien shakes his head yes and takes the man's outstretched hand. They begin to walk to the building, but Damien drops the man's hand and races back to Ace and I. He throws his arms around me and then Ace declaring that we were his bestest friends ever. He then rushes to where his new family is waiting, and they disappear inside. About thirty minutes later, Damien and his new family exit Maxwell Boys Home. Damien turns to us and waves. They all get into the car and are gone.

I turn to Ace beside me and see tears silently trekking down his face. Damien was his best friend. I should have known the loss would be hard on him. I grab him in a fierce hug and try to reassure him. He pushes himself away from me and looks deep into my eyes saying, "It's okay Joey. I'm going to be okay. Jesus is holding me. This is all part of his plan. He has a very different path laid out before me. Joey, my journey is just beginning." I look down at him, and God's plan for my life is revealed to me. I am here only to help Ace on his journey. That day, I vow to do whatever necessary to make sure Ace reaches his full potential and fulfills the plans God has for him.

Preacher John visits us every Sunday, today being no exception. He pulls to a stop in front of the building, and Ace races off to find Gev. We all gather beneath a giant oak tree and Preacher John hands us each a sucker. He looks at us gravely and says, "I'm sorry to be the bearer of bad news, but your father was killed yesterday. He was drunk driving and smashed into another car. The other cars occupants are all okay, but your father was killed on impact. I am truly sorry boys."

I look at him, and sadly I think to myself, "I doubt he will be joining Mama in heaven." To Preacher John I say, "Oh well," and shrugging my shoulders, I walk off. Gev races back to his friends and Ace runs after me. When he comes up beside me, I look down into his clear blue eyes. There isn't a drop of sadness in them. What's sad is the fact that none of us really care that our father is dead. He was already dead to us anyways. Preacher John gets back in his car and drives away. He will be back next Sunday.

Together, Ace and I race toward the basketball court. Ace makes it there first. He picks the ball up shoots. It's a swish, nothing but net. He does a little jig, and I laugh. My tensions drain away. Dad did at least one good thing for us. He brought us to Maxwell Boys Home. He gave us one last shot at happiness, and for that I will always be grateful. I decide then that all three of us will be present at his funeral.

Later that day, I sit Gev and Ace down and try to explain to them why we are attending Dad's funeral. Gev protests loudly, declaring hotly, "He didn't care about us, so why should we care about him?"

To that I say, "He is still our dad, and he did us a favor. He brought us here." That quiets him, and Ace nods his head in silent agreement.

Chapter 7

The day of the funeral dawns bright and clear, but as the day progresses, it becomes dark, gloomy, and oppressive. At 1:00 p.m. on the dot, Preacher John pulls his rusty old car into Maxwell Boys Home's driveway. My brothers and I are dressed to impress. As we climb into Preacher John's car, it begins to rain.

All the way to the church, it pours.

We enter the sanctuary completely soaked. Preacher John ushers us down the aisle and into the front pew.

The funeral starts at 1:30 p.m. Preacher John says a few words and reads from his Bible. He then says a prayer, and everyone is invited to the front where the casket sits open. Gev and I have both been to a funeral before, Mom's, but Ace has never been to one before. I don't know how he will react. We are first in line for the viewing. I stop in front of the casket and look down at the face of my dad. He looks different. Death does that to a person. Ace's hand slips into mine. The rain pounds overhead. A single tear rolls down my cheek. Ace's hand trembles in mine. This is much harder than I thought it would be. As we file out of the sanctuary, the rain falls harder. God is mourning with us. He mourns for another lost soul. We get back into Preacher John's rust bucket and follow the hearse to the cemetery. We walk through the rain to get to the grave site. I watch as my dad's casket is carried and placed on the platform. There are no flowers. Miraculously, the rain stops as the final prayer is said. As we walk from the grave, the sun shines and white, fluffy clouds grace the sky. "God is smiling." Ace declares, pointing up at the sky. I look up to see some clouds have formed in the shape of a smiley face. A rainbow arcs above them, making it look like it has hair. I glance back over my shoulder and see the casket being lowered into the grave. Dad is gone forever, but I smile anyway. Beside me, Ace begins to sing, "This is the day, yes, this is the day that the Lord has made. I will rejoice, I will rejoice and be glad in it…" Preacher John joins in, and soon everyone is singing along. For such a gloomy day, it has ended in such a joyful way.

Ace always finds a way to make every situation a happy one. At the ripe old age of seven, my brother has taught me an important lesson. If you can find the good in everything and everyone then you'll always be happy. It isn't an easy task, but Ace makes it look so simple. We exit the graveyard with smiles on our faces, and I think to myself that we are probably the only group of people in the whole world who smile when leaving a graveyard right after the burial of a loved one.

Back on the road, my smile grows until I burst into fits of laughter. Ace and Gev join in, and I hear Preacher John chuckle lightly to himself.

Back at the Home, we exit Preacher John's car still laughing. The boys outside look our way, probably wondering why we are laughing after just arriving back from our Dad's funeral. They soon lose interest and go back to their activities. Ace sobers up as soon as he realizes that he missed a whole day of school. Gev calls him a nerd and runs out of hitting distance. Ace gives chase. I watch as Ace tackles Gev to the ground and laughingly demand he take it back. Gev, breathing heavily, manages to say, "Never!" I've never seen my brothers so light and carefree. It's nice to see them behaving like little boys should.

Suddenly, Ace is on his feet and running toward the giant oak tree where we usually meet with Preacher John. I run to catch up to him, but he is too far ahead. When I reach the oak, Ace points up into the branches, and I see two glowing yellow eyes peering back at me. It's a cat. "Here kitty, kitty, here kitty, I want hurt you. I'm a friend. I can help you." Ace coos softly to the creature. I watch mesmerized as the cat launches itself into Ace's outstretched arms. I'm too stunned to speak. "It's a girl." He announces happily. I look at the cat. It's just a kitten, I realize, maybe seven to eight weeks old. It's covered with many colors. The colors range from black to brown to yellow to orange all blended together. "She's a tortoiseshell. Tortoiseshells are also known as Calicos. They are always girls. Boy ones are very rare." Ace spouts off the facts like they are common knowledge. Ace looks down at the cat and declares, "I'm going to call her Callie."

By this time, Gev has joined us underneath the tree and points out, "We're not allowed to have pets here, Ace. You know that."

The smile disappears from his face and is replaced with a pout. I feel like punching Gev for his careless words, but I refrain myself. I know that he is right, so I march to Mr. Maxwell's office. I knock softly on the door and am invited in automatically. I tell Mr. Maxwell about the cat, and he agrees to let Ace keep it in the empty shed behind the Home. I rush to inform Ace of the happy news. Upon hearing it, he jumps for joy, literally. Callie sits happily purring in his arms. Ace is great with animals too.

Mrs. Collins takes Ace and I to the store, where I use the rest of my money to buy a food and water bowl and a collar. Mrs. Collins, out of the goodness of her heart, buys a litterbox, litter, a tag, and cat food for our new cat. Once back at the Home, we take all our things back to the shed. Ace fills up the food and water bowls and sets up the litterbox. He puts Callie in the shed, and we turn to leave. Ace suddenly turns back around and opens the small window at the back. "For air," he explains. We leave the shed, shutting the door firmly behind us.

Every day during free period, Ace lets Callie out of the shed. She is never far from his side and watches us as we shoot hoops. She follows us to the water fountain, and when we go back inside, she follows us as well. Ace always scoops her up into his arms and back in the shed she goes. It's like the Mary had a little lamb story but with a cat and a little boy. One day I joked with him saying, "Ace has a little cat, little cat, little cat, Ace has a little cat with tortoiseshell fur. And everywhere that Ace goes his cat is sure to follow." We both burst out laughing at the silly little song.

Chapter 8

Today is my eighteenth birthday. The past five years have really flown by. Things are about to drastically change. Today will be a turning point in our lives. Preacher John pulls into the new parking lot. Over the years, more people have come looking to adopt. Somehow my brothers and I managed to escape it.

I pull Gev and Ace into a group hug, and Gev quickly pushes me away. It would ruin his tough guy image to be caught hugging his big brother. I laugh and ruffle his hair playfully. Ace leans into my embrace. At the age of twelve, he has learned to keep his emotions hidden. He no longer holds my hand or cries in my arms. He isn't that same three-year-old boy anymore. He never tells me what he is thinking. We still shoot hoops every day during free period, but it's much quieter these days. He has taught himself how to play the piano, harmonica, guitar, and flute. He has learned trigonometry, Spanish, and other things way beyond his years. Everything he tries, he is good at. The kid really is an ace, and I couldn't be any more proud of him than I already am.

"I'll be back for you guys." I promise them as I get into Preacher John's new car and wave at them. As we drive away, I can't help thinking that things are never going to be the same. I am optimistic that that is a good thing. As we turn down my old neighborhood, I think of my future instead of my past.

I'm staying with Preacher John until I have a good, steady job and enough money to get my own place. Once I have my feet on the ground so to speak, I plan on getting custody of Gev and Ace. It isn't going to be an easy task, but I plan to accomplish it to the best of my abilities. The rest is up to God. I'll still visit them in the Home until then though.

#

It has been a week since I left the Home. I haven't been to visit my brothers yet because I have nothing good to tell them. I have applied at several places around town, and so far, they have all turned me down. I am becoming discouraged. Today is going to be different. As I walk up the sidewalk to Lowes, I know I can get a job here. I have my application all filled out, and I hand it to a pretty young lady. She smiles at me, and I fumble for something to say. I haven't had much contact with the female gender since living at Maxwell's. I smile and thank her politely, and then I take my leave.

I almost make it out the door before I hear my name being called from behind me. An older gentleman puts out his hand for me to shake as I turn back around. He informs me that he is the manager. He pulls me into his office and tells me to have a seat. I must have missed the part when he told me that this was an interview because he begins to ask me questions. I try to think straight and come up with good answers, but some of them I stumble over because my mind is in a whirl. He concludes the interview by shaking my hand again and declaring, "I'll see you on Monday at 2:00 p.m. sharp. Don't be late."

I got the job. I can't believe I actually got the job. On my way out, I pass the pretty young lady. She smiles and gives me a thumbs up. I wave back and exit the store with a silly grin on my face. Preacher John gave me his old rusty car after I got my license a few days ago. I get in and drive straight to the church. Preacher John must have heard me pull up because when I get out of the car, he is standing there waiting for me. I smile and grab him in a fierce hug yelling, "I got the job," over and over again.

Later that day, I drive out to the Home at a time I know that they'll be in free period. I see Ace first. He is shooting hoops by himself. I inwardly sigh. Not since Damien has he made any new friends. He worries me sometimes. I exit the car. He has yet to see me. Once on the basketball court, I pick up the other ball. I shoot and miss. Ace turns to me and a smile breaks out across his face. I tell him about my new job and getting my license. I tell him about Preacher John generously giving me his old car.

He congratulates me, and we walk over and sit in the grass. It needs to be mowed. When I stand in it, it comes almost to my knees. I am close to six feet tall, so the grass is definitely too high. I feel something rub against me and jump to my feet in surprise. Thinking it is a snake or something, I take a step back. I look down and two pointed ears poke out of the grass. The rest of its body follows. It's Callie. I should have known. The crazy thing still follows Ace everywhere. Gev spots us, and I tell him all my news and then take my leave. I open my car door and then decide that I will mow the yard. Someone should do it. I go to where I know the lawnmower is kept and drag it into the yard. I pull the starter once, twice, three times, and it refuses to start. The gas tank is full, the spark plug is on, and I don't have any idea what could be wrong with it. Ace finds me there, and I explain my problem. He tinkers with the mower for a minute and then pulls the starter. The thing comes to life with a roar, and off I go. It's hard going for a while, but soon I fall into the groove of things. I don't know how much time has gone by, but more than half the yard is finished. Ace comes up to me carrying a glass of water. He hands it to me declaring, "You've been at it for nearly two hours. Let me finish for you." I gladly let him take over. I'm sweating bullets. It is summertime and hotter than blazes out here.

Ace soon finishes and has to get ready for bed. I get into my rusty car and drive back to Preacher John's small house behind the church. My car has no air conditioner, so I roll down all the windows. The air is hot and sticky, but it's better than nothing. As I pull into the church parking lot and cut the engine, I think back to early that day when Ace was mowing the last of the yard. In my mind's eye, I glimpse the tip of two pointed ears, and then the rest of the body emerges. Even while he was mowing, that crazy cat was following him. A lazy smile slowly creeps across my face.

Chapter 9

Monday arrives, and my first day at work begins. I arrive at 2:00 p.m. on the dot. The pretty lady from the other day greets me at the door. "Hello! My name is Lindy, and I'm your trainer for today. You're going to learn to work the cash register." She says cheerfully. My first day goes by in a blur. I don't get to leave until closing at 11:00 p.m., so it's a long day. Lindy's ever-present cheeriness keeps me going though. The rest of the week is much the same as Monday, and I soon fall into the routine of working.

#

It's Sunday, and I have the day off. I go to church with Preacher John, and I praise God for my new job. After the service, I decide to visit my brothers. Ace meets me as I'm getting out of the car. He urges me to hurry up and follow him. He's very excited about something. He brings me to Callie's shed and pulls open the door. He pushes me inside and holds a finger to his lips. He points to a box in a corner of the tiny shed. I slowly make my way to the box. I can hear it now. Tiny squeaks are coming from the box. I look into the box. Four tiny bundles of fur surrounded by Callie's sleek body are in the box. Callie had kittens. Three white kittens with patches of calico and a white and gray kitten make up the litter. Pointing at each kitten in turn, Ace tells me their names are Mary, Laura, Cary, and Todd. Todd is the white and gray kitten and the only boy. Their eyes have yet to open. Ace tells me they were born last Sunday. "You're a Grandfather." I tease him. He beams with pride.

#

Another year has gone by, and I've yet to get my own place. Today is the day. I pull up in front of a rundown piece of property. The yard hasn't been mowed in ages, and the house looks to be falling apart. The place is in complete disarray. I have never seen anything more beautiful. This is my new place. It is cheap and the only thing that I can afford at the moment. I unload my new lawnmower from the back of my new or new used truck, and I get to work.

In no more than two hours, I have the yard mowed completely. I let myself into the house. I look around. It doesn't look too bad. The outside of the house is a different story. It needs a fresh coat of paint, and the windows need a good cleaning. Shutters are hanging haphazardly, and the siding is coming undone. One of the windows is completely missing. I climb back into my truck and head to Lowes for supplies.

Today is my day off, and Lindy will probably wonder why I'm here. Over the past year we have gotten to know each other pretty well. She knows my story and I know hers. We are great friends. When she sees me come in the door, she waves and makes her way over to me. When she reaches me, I sling my arm across her shoulders and declare, "I've bought a house, and I've come for supplies." She smiles sweetly up at me, and we go back to the paint aisle together. She knows what this means for my brothers and me. We will all be together again.

I grab some brown paint and make my way to the other things on my list. I give Lindy directions to the house, and she promises to drop by once she gets off work in an hour.

After leaving Lowes, I drive to Maxwell Boys Home. This time I enter the building and knock on Mr. Maxwell's office door. Gev and Ace are in classes at this time of day along with everyone else, so no one is around. Mr. Maxwell opens the door, and I shake his offered hand. Smiling, he motions me to take a seat. I explain to him that I'm ready to get custody of my brothers. He smiles at me knowingly. He knew this was what I had come for. I sign a few papers and answer a few questions.

Finally, Mr. Maxwell calls over the intercom for Ace and Gev to come to his office. I hear them before I see them. I can hear their feet pounding down the hallway. Sixteen-year-old Gev bursts through the office door first, Ace right behind him. Ace, at five-foot two, didn't stand a chance against Gev's five-foot ten inches. Gev is almost as tall as me, but Ace still has a little growing to do. Once they see me sitting in the office, they high-five each other. They know why I'm here. They are told to pack up their things and meet me at my truck. Once we are all loaded into the crammed seat of my small truck, I start the engine.

On the drive to our new house, I inform them that we have painting to do. When we pull up in front of the house, their mouths fall open. "It looks better than it did." I inform them with a chuckle. Lindy's brand-new Honda is parked in the driveway.

Ace is the first out of the truck. He begins to walk toward Lindy's car, throwing over his shoulder, "Who's here?" Before I can answer him, Lindy exits her car. Ace holds out a hand for her to shake and introduces himself. Lindy smiles and says something that I can't make out and then makes her way toward my truck. I swear the kid never meets a stranger. Gev gets out leaving me alone in the truck wondering why I'm still in there. I open my door and motion for Gev and Ace to unload the truck. The first thing Ace grabs is a giant cat carrier.

Over the year, Callie's kittens have all grown up. Ace kept Todd but found new homes for the others. He opens the carrier and Callie and Todd race out. As they brush past Lindy, she screeches and jumps clear off the ground. Gev and Ace burst into fits of laughter. One look at her face gets me going too. When one Timbermen brother starts to laugh, the other two will always follow.

Lindy marches her five-foot-three-inch self-up to me and punches my arm. She glares up at me and bellows, "Joey Kendall Timbermen, it isn't funny! It was a mouse!" She then proceeds to punch my arm again, but my smile stops her.

She looks around at all three of us and settles on Ace's guilty face. "It was my cats," he manages to get out before more peals of laughter rack his body. She grabs the paint can out of my hand and marches toward the house. We unload the rest of the things and then get started.

I crack open the can of paint and dip my roller in. Everyone else follows suit. We paint until, beside me, Ace's belly growls. It's well past supper. I look over at Ace and see that there is more paint on him than the porch rail he is currently painting. We quickly finish the job. I turn back to Ace, and he slings his dripping paint brush at me. It splatters my shirt. A paint war soon ensues. By the time it's over, we are all splattered with paint. Lindy, declaring she has work tomorrow, takes her leave.

My brothers and I enter the house and get washed up. We change into clean clothes and settle around the rough-hewn kitchen table. I take Gev's and Ace's hands in mine. They clasp hands and we bow our heads. "Thank You for our new home," I start, "and for bringing us together again. I ask you to bless this food and us."

"Thank You for many good years at Maxwell Boys Home," Gev continues, "and for giving me the opportunity at a better life."

"Thank You for always watching over us, especially me because you know I needed watching over. Also, thank you for finally answering my long-ago prayer for a home all my own. We love you God." Ace adds in his innocent voice.

"In Jesus name we pray, Amen." I finish the prayer, and we dig into our frozen dinners. This is the beginning of many more happy days in our very own home.

Chapter 10

We've been living in the house for two months now. It looks better than ever. Gev and Ace have been enrolled in a public school. Every morning, I drive them to Lendrell High School. Every afternoon, the bus brings them back home. They are left to fend for themselves for most of the evening because I don't get home until 9:00 p.m. most nights. I work from 11:00 a.m. to 9:00 p.m. every day but Sunday which is my only off day.

Today when I walk in the door, Ace is all over me. He's excited about something. Finally, he hands me a slip of paper. I slowly read over it. It's a flyer advertising basketball tryouts for a community team. "The gym is just down the block." Ace informs me, "I can walk to it." I read over the flyer again and slowly shake my head in accent. Ace jumps in the air, pumping his fist and shouting, "Yes! Yes! Yes!" I laugh and ruffle his pitch-black hair.

I look around for Gev, but don't see him anywhere. He must be in his room. "Gev hasn't come home yet." Ace tells me, "He didn't ride the bus today." This can't be good. It's after nine, and it's a school night. I hope he hasn't caved into peer pressure or fallen in with the wrong crowd.

I fix Ace and I something to eat and settle down to wait. Ace eventually goes to bed, and I'm left anxiously waiting by myself. At 11:04 p.m., the front door is slowly pushed open. Gev silently enters the living room. I don't move a muscle until he passes my seat on his way down the hall to his room. I jump and tackle him to the floor. His face is pressed to the ground. "Where have you been?" I growl. His breathing is coming in labored gasps. I slowly release my hold and anchor myself off of him. I switch the light on. Light floods the room. I turn back to Gev, standing a few feet away. His nose is bleeding profusely and both eyes are black. He has a busted lip, and it's dripping blood down his shirt. I rush toward him in shock demanding to know what happened to him.

Ace comes out of his room down the hall and stops in his tracks when he sees Gev's face. He goes into the bathroom instead and running water can be heard. Gev still hasn't answered my questions. I glare at him and go into the kitchen. I grab a bag of frozen peas and wrap a hand towel around it. When I reenter the living room, Ace has given Gev a wet rag. I hand Gev the frozen peas and instruct him to start talking.

Gev looks at me in misery and begins, saying, "I hitched a ride with some guys from school who I thought were my friends. They were going to give me a ride home but took me to a junkyard at the edge of town instead. They said to be in their gang I had to get initiated. I didn't even know they were part of a gang. They jumped me. Five or six guys all started punching me. I blacked out after the tenth or twelfth punch was thrown. I came to a couple of hours ago and began the long trek here."

I give him a sympathetic look and clap his shoulder. Gev winces under my touch. I order him to get some sleep. Ace looks my way and then down the hall following Gev's retreating back. Ace starts down the hall after him, and I stop him with a tug on the back of his shirt. He looks back at my worried face and says reassuringly, "It's okay Joey, God's keeping me safe. I wouldn't hang out with those kinds of people anyways, I promise." I pat his shoulder and make my exit. I feel bad for Gev. Today is only Wednesday. He has two more days of school this week, and he will have to face those guys sometime.

#

The rest of the week goes by without incident. Gev successfully avoids the boys who beat him up, and today is Saturday. Ace is getting ready for his tryouts. I won't be able to go with him because of work, but Gev has promised to take him.

When I get home from work later that night, Ace is watching TV. When I shut the door behind me, he jumps from his seat. With a huge grin on his face, he declares, "I made the team!" I never doubted it.

Over dinner, I am informed that the team is called the Bravehearts, and there are thirteen other boys and girls besides Ace on the team. "You'll never guess who's on the team." Ace says excitedly. He waits all of ten seconds for me to think about it before blurting out, "Damien!" I laugh and ruffle his hair. He grins, and Gev chuckles.

#

Over the next few weeks, Damien and Ace become fast friends again. Damien goes to Lendrell High as well. He comes over to our house every day after practice. It's good to see him again. Ace is made team captain of the Bravehearts and loves every minute of it. So far, they have had two games, and Ace has led them to victory both games. All his teammates have become some of his best friends. He loves playing ball for a team, and I love to see him so happy.

Chapter 11

Today is Saturday and I have the day off. A few more years have gone by, but nothing has really changed. I am twenty-three but fill forty. Ace is turning seventeen in a couple of days, and Gev is already twenty and graduated from high school.

Ace is in his senior year. He is what some people would label popular, but really all the popular kids just come to him for homework help and tutoring. He has started a book club and made several friends through it. Clifford, Talon, Craig, Minnie, and Georgia, make up the members of the book club. Damien, of course, is in it too.

Every year for the past four years, Ace and Damien have played basketball on the Braveheart's team. They have had a different coach just about every year, and this year the coach is Kevin Martlin. The assistant coach is Shortie Ray. Today, I decide to go watch Ace practice. Kevin is in his late twenties, and he use to play pro ball. He got kicked off his team for smart mouthing the coach. Shortie played pro with him and left when Kevin did.

I walk into the gym and immediately realize that something is wrong. Kevin's face is red as a beet, and he is yelling at Ace and Damien. They are standing their ground though and yelling right back at him. "You can't bench me! You need me to win Monday's game, and you know it. I'm late for one practice, and you lose it. Get a hold of yourself man!" Ace yells at Kevin. Before I can intervene, Ace grabs Damien's arm and stalks away from Kevin saying, "Come on Damien, let's get out of here." I silently applaud my little brother. He handled that better than I probably would have. Ace joins me, and we all walk out together. "I'm reporting him to the board." Ace hotly declares. I don't blame him. I would report him too if I was in his position.

Before we make it to the car, another young man comes storming out of the gym door toward us. He has a short wry frame and a shock of reddish orange hair. He also has some muscle. The guy couldn't be more than five-two. Ace, who has yet to catch up to Gev and me in height, still towers over the guy. I remember seeing him in the previous games. I believe they introduced him as Garfield. The name fits him. Ace takes after our mom in the height department. He is only five-six where Gev and I are both close to six foot. This guy is a year older than Ace, but a lot smaller than him. Once he catches up to us, he glares at Ace with undisguised hatred. He clearly has it in for Ace, I can tell. He shakes his fist in Ace's face declaring, "This isn't over," and stalks away. I look at Ace for an explanation, and he gives me a "let's not go there" look. We then proceed to load into my truck.

Upon arriving home, I find to my chagrin that my girlfriend Lindy is there. I completely forgot about our lunch date that was supposed to be at 12:30 p.m., and it is already after one. I slap my forehead, and Ace and Damien burst out laughing. I glare at them before quickly exiting the truck. Lindy is sitting on the porch swing. Gev is at work, so before he left, he most likely locked the door. There is no telling how long she has been sitting out here waiting for me. I breathe a huge sigh of relief when she greets me with a smile. She isn't mad which is great. I apologize profusely, and then head back to my truck. Ace and Damien have made themselves scarce which is good. They can take care of themselves for a while.

#

At Ace's next practice, Kevin and Shortie are no longer there. A new coach, named Kayden Roberts, has taken their place. This coach is much more laid back and easy going. Actually, he is rarely ever there. Ace has had to step in more often than not to coach the team. As team captain, he feels it's his job to get his teammates ready for the games. I feel that Kayden should be reported too, but Ace doesn't agree. He says that if they have to replace another coach that they'll just shut down the whole team. I decide it's best if I don't interfere.

One day, Ace comes home from practice with a black eye. I don't handle it too well. I literally fly off my rocker. He quickly explains that Garf punched him for trying to be coach. I grab my ever-present bag of frozen peas from the freezer and slap it on his eye. He yelps at the sudden coldness and pain my actions caused. I smile apologetically.

Gev comes into the room and laughs when he sees the peas pressed to Ace's eye. He isn't very sympathetic. I send him a withering look, and he rushes from the room. I turn back to Ace and come to the conclusion that I was right. That Garf guy does have it in for Ace. At eighteen, Ace no longer feels that he needs my help. I feel differently on the subject, but I decide to let him fight this battle on his own because if I get involved it won't be pretty.

#

Basketball season is over, and Ace won't be able to play next season. Eighteen is the age limit. At this time next year, he will be nineteen. Damien and Ace are going out to celebrate the end of the season together, and

Gev has a date. Lindy and I have plans for tonight. She doesn't know it yet, but tonight I'm planning to propose. I'm extremely nervous. Ace knows what I'm planning. As he's going out the door, he sees my panicked face and pats my shoulder reassuringly, saying, "It's okay Joey, if she's the one God has picked out for you then she'll say yes."

I look deep into his bright blue eyes and determine that he's smart about everything. "You know everything don't you." I tease him.

He looks calmly back at me and says, "Not everything, Joey." I think the comment odd at the time but don't question it. I have an important date to get to, and I quickly forget about his odd comment.

Later that night, I ask Lindy to marry me, and like Ace said, she says yes. A year from that day, we are married. I'm the luckiest man alive. A few days later, Ace comes skidding into the house all out of breath. "I'm the new coach and Damien's my assistant." He pants still out of breath. He is excited, and I am excited for him. To celebrate, Lindy cooks Ace's favorite meal, dessert included. Gev has moved into his own place, but Ace still lives with Lindy and I. Ace's cats, Callie and Todd, still take up residence in our backyard. I'm not looking forward to the day that Ace moves out. I guess I'll survive though because I have Lindy now.

Ace is coaching kids age's five to eight. He calls his team the Little Wizards. I love it. There are fourteen kids on the team, and they all adore him.

Today is Friday, and Ace has practice. Lindy and I are relaxing on our day off. She is a preschool teacher now. I still work at Lowes. We are watching a movie, when Ace bursts through the front door. I hear an excited yap coming from inside his jacket. He pulls a little puppy out and hands it to me saying, "My friends, Jamison and Julian's dad was going to kill it because it's the runt of the litter. It's a full-blooded boxer, but it won't get as big as most. I named him Runt." I look down at the puppy in my hands, and the impact of Ace's actions hit me. He saved this little dog's life.

Thus began Ace's animal obsession. He volunteers every day after practice at the local animal shelter now. By the end of the year, he has four dogs plus the two cats he already had. At the end of the year, he also moves out.

Chapter 12

When Ace leaves and gets his own place, my whole world doesn't shatter like I imagined. Ace is still at my house more often than not, but he doesn't sleep here anymore. Ace is twenty years old and able to take care of himself. I tell myself that he no longer needs me, but it doesn't seem to help. The day he moves out, I tell him that he doesn't need me anymore. He quickly reassures me by saying, "I will always need you. No matter how old I get, I will still need you." I hug him close and then release him. I ruffle his hair and shoo him out the door. He's probably too old for me to do that, but he lets me do it anyways.

#

Ace has been living at his own place for a couple of months now. I've been over there a few times, and it's a decent place. It has a large fenced-in yard for his dogs to romp around in. The house is small but perfect for him and his cats to stay in. He is renting it for now, but eventually he hopes to own it.

Since the two months he has been living on his own, he has been seeing a girl. Today, he is bringing her over for dinner at 6:00 p.m. to meet us. Lindy is making spaghetti. At 5:30 p.m., Ace enters the house. I go to the door to greet his date and him. She's a pretty petite little thing. She has the biggest brown eyes I have ever seen and rich chocolate brown hair that hangs past her shoulders, all the way down her back. She can't be taller than five foot. She probably doesn't even weigh a hundred pounds. I look to Ace for an introduction and catch him looking down into the girl's upturned face. The look in his eyes is like none I have ever seen. It's adoring but much more than that too. The look in his eyes as he looks at her is one of pure love.

My little brother is in love.

I hate to break their connection but do it anyways. I loudly clear my throat to get their attention, and the connection is broken. Ace smiles sheepishly at me and says, "Joey, this is Maddie. Maddie, this is my oldest brother Joey and his wife Lindy." I reach out to clasp her outstretched hand. It's so small. She reminds me of a pixie, so tiny and fragile. I look at her and quickly release her hand. Ace looks at me funny but says nothing as we all gather around the dining table. We join hands and ask the blessing with Ace piping in now and then as well. We then begin to dig in.

Everyone gets large helpings of Lindy's amazing spaghetti. Maddie eats less than half of what's on her plate. She says nothing throughout the meal unless someone says something to her directly. She's a quiet one. When Maddie and Ace take their leave, I give Ace a one-sided hug. Maddie holds out her hand for me to shake. I forgo the hand and pull her into a gentle brotherly hug.

A few days later, when Ace shows up at my house, I push him into a chair. "You love her, don't you?" I ask him.

"I don't know." He mumbles awkwardly.

"The look in your eyes says otherwise." I tell him.

He looks down at his hands self-consciously. Several minutes elapse before he looks back up at me. I can tell by the look of wonder on his face that he has come to the same realization that I have. He just realized that he does love her. I clap him on the shoulder and leave him to his thoughts. I have to go to work. Before I can make my exit, Ace stops me with his words. "Do you think she loves me too?" He asks.

I turn back to him. He hasn't moved from where I left him, and he isn't even looking my way. I don't have the answer to his question. The only way for him to find out is to ask her. "Ask her." I finally answer him and walk out the door.

#

Apparently, she returns his feelings because a few months after our conversation, he asks her to marry him. She says yes. When Ace tells me the news, I nearly lose it. My little brother is engaged. Ace is no longer a little boy. He is now a twenty-one-year-old man engaged to be married. I can't believe how the years have passed so quickly. When Ace is gone, I break down in my living room floor. I weep in happiness because after all the bad in our lives, my brothers and I are all happy today.

My happiness is short-lived though because the next day, bad news is delivered to my doorstep. A member of Helpful Hands Church of God knocks on my door.

"Preacher John passed away last night in his sleep. He went in peace…" I am informed upon opening my door. The guy continues to talk, but I don't hear what he's saying. I'm in a daze it seems like. A fog surrounds me. If feels like my ears are clogged with water or cotton balls. I shake the news off convincing myself that it isn't true.

After the guy is gone, I stand there with the door open, not seeing or hearing anything going on around me. Lindy's sweet voice penetrates through the fog surrounding me. "Who was at the door?" She asks. She sounds like she could be miles away, but she is standing right behind me. I turn around and see her beautiful face, and my legs turn to jelly beneath me. They give out under me, and she tries to catch me. I fall to my knees. I begin to shake all over. Lindy crouches down in front of me and wraps her arms around me. Tears begin streaming down my face unchecked.

"Preacher John is gone. "I manage to choke out. She pats my back in comforting circles. I think of Ace and wonder who will do his wedding now.

#

"Preacher John was a good man. He helped my brothers and me when we were all alone and no one else would or could. He cared for us when everyone else stopped caring. He was a great man of God. Preacher John was a good friend, my best friend. They will welcome him in heaven…" As I address the crowd gathered for Preacher John's funeral, I think over all he's done for me. God is smiling today. It's sunshiny and cloudless outside. God is happy to receive Preacher John into His Kingdom today. My brothers and I sit on the first pew. We are the closest thing to family that Preacher John ever had. I look down into the congregation, and my eyes land on the back pew, the pew where my brothers and I spent every Sunday when we were just boys. A little boy sits there today with his mother. I smile and end my speech as I see the boy fidget uncomfortably. I remember being that age. I remember restraining Ace as he fidgeted in that very pew. Everyone is smiling. This is the way Preacher John would have wanted it.

Chapter 13

Eight months have passed since the day Ace got engaged. Today is his wedding day. He has made me his best man. Gev and Damien are groomsmen.

Maddie and Ace decided to have an outdoor ceremony. It's beautiful. Everywhere I look, I see white daises and blue ribbons. The weather is bright and sunny and hot. It's the middle of July, and today is a scorcher.

I look at Ace standing beside me in his pressed tuxedo and blue tie. His smile encompasses his entire face. His eyes are bright and clear. He doesn't seem even the teeniest bit nervous. He looks happy and excited.

The wedding march begins, and Maddie comes gliding down the aisle on her father's arm. She is stunning in a beautiful white dress that flows across the ground behind her. I look over at Ace to catch his reaction. Tears glisten in his once clear eyes. I turn back to see Maddie as she gets closer to the front. She looks even more like a fairy than before.

I started calling her Pixie a few months ago, and the name has stuck. We have all started referring to her as that now. Pixie's father hands her off to Ace, and their vows are said. "I now pronounce you husband and wife. You may kiss your bride." The minister announces. Ace lifts the veil from Pixie's face and kisses his bride. Cheers erupt all around. Pixie and Ace turn to the audience and begin the trek back down the aisle.

The ceremony is over. My little brother is a married man now. I can hardly believe it. A tear slips from my eye, and I quickly wipe it away before anyone can see. I'm not quick enough though because Gev sees me and gives me a knowing smile.

#

This past year has flown by. I haven't seen nearly as much of Ace as I'm used to, but he is married now, so that makes sense. Today is Ace's twenty-third birthday. We are celebrating at his house. Pixie is throwing him a party. Lindy and I are the last to arrive. Gev is already there. Pixie's parents are there as well.

The party goes off without a hitch. Everyone is having a good time. Ace yells to get everyone's attention. When everyone is focused on Pixie and him standing in the center of the room, he says, "We have an announcement to make." He then motions for Pixie to speak. "We're having a baby!" She exclaims excitedly. My mouth drops open. My little brother is going to be a daddy. I can't believe that he's going to be a daddy before I am.

#

Since the day of Ace's party, five months have passed. Pixie is seven months into her pregnancy. Her belly is round and huge. She looks deathly ill. Ace tells me that her doctor is worried. The doctor says that she shouldn't have been able to get pregnant, ever, and that it will be difficult for her to deliver. They will probably have to do a C-section. She probably won't be able to go her full term. At the beginning, the doctor tried to convince them to get an abortion because of all the risk involved in her carrying the baby to full term. He told them that it could kill her. Pixie and Ace agreed to go ahead and have the baby.

Today is Sunday. I'm sitting in my recliner when the phone rings. I grab it off the hook on the table beside me and answer it. "Pixie's gone into labor. We're at the hospital." Ace informs me in a panic.

"I'm on my way." I try to assure him. I hang up the phone and grab my wallet and keys on my way out the door. I get into my truck and turn the ignition. It won't start. "Come on. Come on." I pray. I try it again, and the engine sputters to life. I drive as quickly as possible without breaking the law. I arrive at the hospital in no time.

Pixie is two months early which can't be a good thing. With this thought in mind, I take the stairs two at a time up to the delivery ward. I pray the whole time. I finally burst through the waiting room doors. Ace is pacing like a caged tiger ready to pounce on the first unsuspecting victim he can find which just so happens to be me. He sees me and comes rushing to my side exclaiming, "They won't let me be with her. It must be bad Joey. They've been in there forever. What am I supposed to do?"

I grasp his hands firmly in mine and simply say, "Pray. Pray is all you can do. One way or another, she's going to be okay." I guide him to a chair and gently push him into it. His head hangs limply in his hands. I can't tell if he is praying, but I begin to pray aloud.

How long we sit there like that, I have no idea. What could have been hours or just minutes go by before the doctor enters the waiting area. We don't see or hear him at first. "Excuse me." He says. Ace's head snaps up, and my praying ceases. I look around me and notice Gev and Pixie's parents are there with us. I look at the doctor and see the grim look on his face. Knowing the news isn't going to be good, I grab Ace's arm in restraint. Gev moves to his other side and takes that arm. "I'm sorry…" the doctor trails off and then continues, "We weren't able to save her. She was already so weak." The doctor motions to someone out in the hall.

I brace Ace against the chair. He strains against my arm. He tries to break free. I know what he wants. He wants to charge into the delivery room to see for himself that she is gone. "She's gone Ace. Do you hear me? I said she's gone." I yell at him. I don't know if he is able to hear me through the fog that I know has descended over him. He is in a daze. His eyes have taken on a glassy look. I begin to shake him. In my peripheral vision, I see a nurse enter the room. I hear wailing.

It's a baby. The nurse has a baby.

The wail must have pierced through Ace's fog because he suddenly heaves against my arms and breaks free. He runs to the baby. I try to stop him. The doctor says something to him, and he falls to his knees with tears spilling down his face. I rush to his side and grab him in my arms. As we rock back and forth, he whispers over and over again, "The baby's okay. He's okay." I slowly release Ace as he clambers to his feet. He says something in a low voice to the nurse, and she hands him the baby.

I watch as my brother looks down into the eyes of his newborn child. All the love he had for Pixie is reflected in his eyes as he looks at his son. I slowly approach him and look down at my new nephew. He isn't wailing anymore. The wailing stopped as soon as he was transferred to his daddy's arms. Tears are still streaming down Ace's face, silently. Ace looks up at the people gathered in the room and announces, "Everyone meet, Arthur Benjamin Timbermen." He smiles through his tears.

The doctor motions for Ace to come with him. Ace hands me tiny Arthur and follows the doctor out. I look down into Arthur's innocent baby face. "He's going to do great things one day." I think to myself, "He's one special baby boy."

We all follow Ace and the doctor down the hall. The doctor motions us into a dimly lit delivery room. Pixie's unmoving body is lying on the bed. Ace rushes to her lifeless side. His body is racked with sobs. My heart breaks for my brother. Mom died giving birth to Ace, and now Ace's wife has died giving birth to his son. It's a vicious cycle and all terribly unfair. I watch as my brother's life seems to come crashing in on him.

I remember when Mom died, and Dad pulled away from us. I remember going to Dad's funeral and then Preacher John's. My brothers and I have had a tough life. We have experienced more heartache in a short amount of time than anyone else that I know. We are all still alive and healthy which is one thing to be thankful for.

I look down into Arthur's face. He is another thing to give thanks for, perhaps the biggest thing to give thanks for.

Chapter 14

Ace and I are relaxing on my front porch swing. I watch as two-year-old Arthur rolls around in my front yard. He has grown a lot. He turns three in a few weeks. I can't believe how the years have flown by. Arthur goes everywhere with Ace. He especially likes going to practice with him. He loves to watch his daddy coach. One day, Ace will teach him how to play basketball, but for now he is content to just watch him grow. The love Ace has for his son shines in his eyes. Arthur looks just like his daddy with his bright curious blue eyes and pitch-black hair. The resemblance is uncanny.

Lindy and I have decided to adopt. I'm waiting for her to get home as I sit here with Ace. We are going today. Maxwell Boys Home has been closed down, so we will have to go somewhere else to adopt. I look over at Ace. I can tell that he is deep in thought. "One day, I'm going to open a refuge for kids. I believe it's my calling." He says quietly. I know he's serious. I also believe that it's a great idea and tell him so.

Lindy finally arrives, and we head off to find the new member or members of our family. We have been trying for several years to have a baby of our own, but she just hasn't been able to conceive. We decided to give up and just adopt. We pull into Copelend Orphanage, and I spot them almost instantly, a little boy and girl lying on their backs in the grass. They remind me of Ace and me on the day that Damien got adopted. I point them out to Lindy, and she immediately falls in love with them. They introduce themselves as Morgan and Chase. They are six-year-old twins. They come home with us that very day. They become the newest members of the Timbermen family.

#

It has been two weeks since the twins have come to live with us. Today is Thursday, and Ace has practice. He took Arthur with him. He usually does. I'm taking the twins for ice cream, and as they are getting their shoes on, a knock comes at the door. The knocking becomes louder and more persistent until it is practically a bang. I throw open the door ready to give whoever it is what's for. I take one look at my visitor and change my mind. It's Damien, and he is covered from head to toe in soot and ashes. The smell of smoke permeates the air around him. It is overpowering. It's not his appearance that lets me know that something is terribly wrong but the look in his eyes.

"Someone set the gym on fire." He says, "We were in the middle of practice when we smelled the smoke, and then the fire alarm went off. Flames popped up out of nowhere, and we rushed to get everyone out safely. We made it out of the building, but Arthur wasn't with us. By that time firemen had arrived, but Ace wouldn't get their help. Flames were licking at the building, and Ace ran right into it. I tried to stop him, but he refused to listen to reason. He kept insisting that he wasn't going to lose Arthur too. I waited and waited for him to reemerge, but it had already been fifteen minutes. I was getting worried, so I got the attention of the closest fireman and told him what was going on. He spoke quickly into his radio, and several men rushed into the burning building. I waited for what seemed like hours but in all reality were mere minutes when they finally emerged from the building. It collapsed behind them. I rushed toward them. One was carrying the small form of Arthur and two others were carrying the still form of Ace. They were both placed on stretchers and carried off in an ambulance. I asked the firemen if they were going to be okay, and they told me that it didn't look good. They wanted me to go to the hospital to be checked out as well, but I rushed over here straight away to let you know. I'm so sorry Joey."

I call to the twins and punch speed dial on my phone. Lindy picks up on the second ring. I quickly fill her in, and she promises to let Gev know. She will meet us at the hospital. I push Damien and the twins out the door and into my car. I rush toward the hospital not caring about the speed limit. I pray fervently the entire time. A siren penetrates through my prayers. A police cruiser is behind me. I'm going seventy in a thirty-five miles-per-hour zone. I pull over and roll down my window. The officer strides toward us and pulls out a notepad. He takes one look at my panicked face and asks, "Is everything okay sir?"

I feel like screaming. I rest my head against the steering wheel for a minute to calm myself down then look up at the officer. "No Officer, everything is not okay. My brother has been in a terrible fire. He is in critical condition, and I would like to make it to the hospital before it's too late." As I talk, I feel my voice rising with every word.

The officer's eyes cloud with sympathy, and he reaches out for my hand. When our hands connect, he latches on firmly. "May I pray with you son?" He asks me. I nod my head in accent. He closes his eyes and bows his head. I follow suit. "Heavenly Father, we come to you today to ask for your healing and mercy on behalf of my young friend's brother. Please watch over him and wrap him in your warm secure embrace. Let him know that he is not alone. Dear Father, watch over his family in this time of uncertainty and put their minds at ease to the fate of their loved one. I ask this in Jesus name, Amen." He prays.

Tears begin streaming down my face, and I am powerless to stop them. A knot is clogging my throat, and I can't speak, so I just nod my thanks. The police officer offers to escort us to the hospital, and we make it there in record time. I fly through the hospital doors with Damien and the twins just a few steps behind me. I ask the nurse at the front desk which way to go, and she leads me to a room on the first floor. I walk in and see Arthur sitting up in the bed. I rush to him and fold him in my arms. He looks okay. Another nurse enters and tells me that Arthur is free to go. He only has a few scratches. There isn't a single burn on him. That is a miracle in and of itself. I thank God for it.

I ask the nurse about Ace, and she directs us to a waiting area outside of the Emergency room. She tells us that a doctor will be in shortly to inform us of Ace's condition. Once we sit down, I look at Arthur. He looks confused. "What's going on Uncle Joey? What are we still here for?" He asks me in his little boy voice. He doesn't know.

I pull him onto my lap and hold his small head to my chest. I stroke his hair in a soothing motion. I try to tell him in little boy terms about his daddy and what happened. "You were in a fire buddy, and your daddy went in to save you. You're okay, but your daddy isn't so good. God is watching over him, though, so don't worry. Everything is going to be okay."

Tears begin streaming down his face as he asks, "Where is my daddy Uncle Joey? Is he going to die?"

I pull him closer, murmuring, "I don't know pal. I just don't know."

#

Lindy and Gev soon join us in the waiting area. I tell them about the fire and the police officer. Hours go by before the doctor in his white lab coat enters the room. Arthur is asleep in the chairs beside me. I surge to my feet, and he sits up groggily, rubbing his eyes. I rush toward the doctor. He's already shaking his head. "Your brother is in very critical condition. He has several major burns, and he isn't breathing on his own. We have him hooked to a breathing machine, but we can't keep him on it indefinitely. We don't think he's going to last much longer. You guys may go in one at a time to say your goodbyes. He will be able to hear you, but he may not be able to respond." The doctor informs us gravely and leads us to Ace's room.

I hold myself back and let the others go before me. The fog has descended, this time much worse than before.

My mind travels back over everything we've been through. The good and the bad times flash in my memory. Ace as a little boy no older than Arthur being slapped by Dad, Ace clinging to my hand our first day at Maxwell Boys Home not wanting me to leave him, Ace teaching himself anything and everything, his contagious excitement at the library, his joy over Callie and her kittens, Ace telling Kevin off, and finally, Ace holding baby Arthur in his arms as his world shatters around him. I can't believe it's going to end like this.

Finally, I'm the only one left to see him. I try to brace myself for what I'm about to see. It doesn't work. I step into the room and see Ace's scarred face and prone body. An oxygen mask is covering his nose and mouth. He is hooked to lots of machines. I collapse to my knees beside the bed, begging God for mercy. I can't bear to let him go. I can't bear to see my little brother this way. I grab his hand in mine. Tears are streaming down my face. Through my agony, I don't hear anything until Ace's hand tightens around mine. I look up and place my ear close to his mouth. He brings his other hand up to touch my face and says in a raspy, quiet voice, "It's okay Joey. Don't cry. God is holding me. I'm ready to join him in Heaven. My time is up. My destiny has been fulfilled. This isn't goodbye. This is see you soon. Take good care of Arthur. Take care of him like you took care of me all those years. Don't let him grieve too much. He deserves to be a little boy for as long as he can. I love you Joey." His hand falls from my face.

My tears begin anew, and they aren't silent anymore. I watch through blurred vision as Ace takes a breath and then is still. I grasp his limp hand tighter in mine and will him to come back, to wake up. He doesn't stir. He's gone.

#

A few days later after the funeral is over, Damien tells me that Garf was the one who set fire to the gym. He was taken to jail and will be there for a very long time. I pray God will help me to forgive Garf one day. I vow to not hold a grudge, but it's hard not to do. I visit Garf in jail a few times. I try to tell him about God. He tells me that he didn't know any one was in the gym that day. After my fourth visit he gives his life to the Lord. I am finally able to forgive him. It will be even harder for him to forgive himself.

I continue to visit Garf in jail. I've taken him under my wing. Ace would have wanted it that way because that was just the kind of person that he was. He had a big heart and was always willing to help those in need, whether it be physical or spiritual.

Epilogue

"So you see guys, you didn't get to know your uncle Ace very well, but he was a good man. Arthur is still grieving, and you were having fun at his expense. That wasn't a very nice thing to do." I say as my story comes to an end. I look into the twins eyes and see deep remorse. I look over at Arthur. Tears are flowing down his face.

It has only been six months since Ace's passing. It's still hard to talk or even think about it. I know he's in a better place, but that doesn't mean I don't miss him something terrible. I feel like a failure. All those years ago, I promised myself and God that I would watch over Ace and make sure that he fulfilled his destiny. I know he told me that he had, but it doesn't seem like it to me. I failed.

Sometime during the story Lindy went outside and got the mail. Now, she hands me a piece of it. It has Ace's name on it. I slowly tear it open and pull out a letter. It's a letter confirming the purchase of the building Maxwell Boys Home was in. I read over the letter several times before it sinks in, and my plan takes root.

#

A month has come and gone, and today is the big day. I look out into the sea of faces there for the grand opening. Arthur is smiling beside me as I hand him the scissors. The countdown begins, "5, 4, 3, 2, 1." Arthur snaps the red ribbon. I guide a group of four or five children through the open gate, saying loud enough for all to hear, "Welcome to Ace's Refuge!"

The entire town it seems has turned out for this event. It is heartening to see so many there in support. I stand by the door welcoming everyone in. There is only one guy left. He clasps my hand in his and says, "There is something you should know son. I'm a fireman, and I was at the fire that claimed you brother's life. I was the guy who found him in that burning building. Your brother is a hero. When I found him he was shielding that little boy's body with his own. He had taken his shirt off and had it held over the boy's nose and mouth. He saved his life. You should be very proud of your brother."

"That boy is my brother's son." I say with tears in my eyes, "Thank you for telling me."

I guess Ace fulfilled his destiny after all. He sacrificed his life for the life of his child, just like Jesus sacrificed his for us. Sometimes, a person's destiny isn't what you might think it should be. Sometimes, it's even greater than you could have imagined. I wonder what my destiny is. I believe that only God knows that.

www.ingramcontent.com/pod-product-compliance
Lightning Source LLC
Chambersburg PA
CBHW070450170726
48291CB00005B/1694
9781951472016